# TIME BLASTERS

# T. REX VS ROBO-DOG 3000

D1111852

Librarian Reviewer
Katharine Kan
Graphic novel reviewer and Library Consultant, Panama City, FL
MLS in Library and Information Studies, University of Hawaii at
Manoa, HI

Reading Consultant
Elizabeth Stedem
Educator/Consultant, Colorado Springs, CO
MA in Elementary Education, University of Denver, CO

STONE ARCH BOOKS
www.stonearchbooks.com

Graphic Sparks are published by Stone Arch Books,
A Capstone Imprint
1710 Roe Crest Drive
North Mankato, Minnesota 56003
*www.capstonepub.com*

*Library of Congress Cataloging-in-Publication Data*
Nickel, Scott.
    T. rex vs Robo-Dog 3000 / by Scott Nickel; illustrated by Enrique Corts.
    p. cm. — (Graphic Sparks.Time Blasters)
    ISBN 978-1-4342-0761-6 (library binding)
    ISBN 978-1-4342-0857-6 (paperback)
    1. Graphic novels. [1. Graphic novels. 2. Time travel—Fiction. 3. Robots—Fiction.
4. Tyrannosaurus rex—Fiction. 5. Dinosaurs—Fiction.] I. Corts, Enrique, ill. II. Title.
III. Title: Tyrannosaurus rex versus Robo-dog three thousand.
PZ7.7.N53Ty 2009
[Fic]—dc22                                      2008006714

Summary: David's brother, Darrin, just invented a radio-controlled pooch. It performs
tricks, mixes delicious smoothies, and grows 50 feet tall. When David's friend brings back
a T. rex from the past, Robo-Dog 3000 turns into the ultimate fighting machine. It's beast
versus bot in the smackdown of the century!

Art Director: Heather Kindseth
Graphic Designer: Brann Garvey

Printed in the United States of America.
3357

# TIME BLASTERS

# T.REX VS ROBO-DOG 3000

by Scott Nickel

illustrated by Enrique Corts

# CAST OF CHARACTERS

Ben

David

Darrin

Brendan

Lisa

Robo-Dog
3000

Another invention?! Wasn't creating a time machine enough?

A scientist never rests, little brother.

I've worked on this three months straight. I haven't even hung out with my girlfriend.

Because you don't have one.

She happens to be an Egyptian princess from the year 2000 B.C.

Now, behold the product of my genius!

Robo-Dog 3000 is online!

Cool! But what can it do?

Robo-Dog performs all the tricks of a normal dog.

Plus, it mixes up delicious smoothies!

WHRR

Mmmm! Tangy!

I call him Rex. Here's the best part. With a simple push of a button . . .

It grows into Ultimate Robo-Dog!

Woof! Woof!

That's awesome, big brother!

Yeah, but you can't tell Mom or Dad or your friends at school.

Rex is top secret!

Who would I tell? My best friend won't even talk to me.

The next day after school . . .

Come on, David! Brendan is taking everyone to see dinosaurs. Real dinosaurs!

Dinosaurs are extinct. They only existed in the past.

Duh, he's taking us back in time! It only costs five dollars.

There's only one way to travel through time, and only I know about it. Oh, and my ex-best friend.

Uh-oh.

Ben! Brendan! Stop!

Here comes Mister "Only I Can Use The Time Machine Controller."

Suddenly . . .

It's a T. rex!

ROOAR

That's correct!

T. rex, or Tyrannosaurus rex. It's one of the largest meat eaters that ever lived—

Stop with the science lesson, and get us out of here!

Meanwhile, David and Ben still continue arguing . . .

And another thing, if you hadn't been so—

WHUMP!

Whoa!

Hey!

I don't believe it! This is bad. Really bad.

What are we gonna do?

My brother will know how to stop the T. rex!

At a nearby park . . .

27

CHOMP

Oh, no! The T. Rex wrecked Robo-Dog!

Well, that wasn't supposed to happen.

Yikes!

Mommy!

Now what?

Don't look at me. You're the one who always wants to be the boss.

# ABOUT THE AUTHOR

Growing up, Scott Nickel wanted to be a comic book writer or a mad scientist. As an adult, he gets to do both. In his secret literary lab, Scott has created more than a dozen graphic novels for Stone Arch Books featuring time travelers, zombies, robots, giant insects, and mutant lunch ladies. Scott's *Night of the Homework Zombies* received the 2007 Golden Duck award for Best Science Fiction Picture Book. When not creating crazy comics, Scott squeezes in a full-time job as a writer and editor at Jim Davis's Garfield studio. He lives in Muncie, Indiana, with his wife, two teenage sons, and an ever-growing number of cats.

# ABOUT THE ILLUSTRATOR

Enrique (ehn-REE-kay) Corts became a professional illustrator at age 19, working on short stories for a Spanish comic magazine. After finishing his art studies, he entered the graphic design and advertising world, spending endless hours chained to his computer. Later, he worked as a concept artist in Great Britain on video games such as *Worms 3D, EyeToy Play 3,* and *Play 4.*

Enrique lives in Palma de Mallorca, Spain. Enrique thinks perhaps someday he will go back to his native Valencia in his quest for more sunlight.

# GLOSSARY

**Cretaceous Period** (kri-TAY-shush PIHR-ee-uhd)—a period of time about 144 to 65 million years ago

**Egyptian** (ee-JIP-shuhn)—often refers to an ancient person from the country of Egypt in northeast Africa

**extinct** (ek-STINGKT)—something that no longer exists; dinosaurs no longer exist, so they are extinct

**herbivores** (HUR-buh-vorz)—animals that eat plants for food instead of eating meat

**invention** (in-VENT-shuhn)—a completely new and original product or idea

**Jurassic Age** (juh-RA-sik AYJ)—a period of time about 206 to 144 million years ago, when many dinosaurs roamed Earth

**PB&J** (P B AND J)—slang term for peanut butter and jelly

**triceratops** (trye-SER-uh-tops)—a large, plant-eating dinosaur with three horns and a fan-shaped collar of bone

**tyrannosaurus** (ti-RAN-uh-sor-uhs)—a large meat-eating dinosaur that walked on its hind legs, also known as T. rex

# MORE ABOUT TYRANNOSAURUS REX

Did you know the scientific name Tyrannosaurus rex (ti-RAN-uh-sor-uhs REX) means "Tyrant Lizard King?" Weighing 5 to 7 tons, this dino certainly was reptile royalty. Here are a few more facts about this giant beast.

The T. rex was the star of the movie *Jurassic Park.* But these dinos didn't actually live during the Jurassic Age. They lived between 65 to 85 million years ago during a time known as the **Cretaceous Period** (kri-TAY-shush PIHR-ee-uhd).

At 40 feet (12 meters) long and 20 feet (6 meters) tall, the T. rex was one of the largest meat-eating dinos.

Although the T. rex was big, that doesn't mean it was slow. Some scientists believe these beasts could chase down their prey at more than 40 miles (64 kilometers) per hour.

For such a large beast, the T. rex's arms were surprisingly small. At only 3 feet (1 meter) long, they were too short to capture prey.

Instead of grabbing prey with its tiny arms, T. rex grabbed food with its teeth. Each T. rex tooth measured more than 9 inches (23 centimeters) long! That's the size of a large banana.

T. rex used its giant teeth to satisfy a giant appetite. With one bite, scientists believe the T. rex could gobble up about 500 pounds of meat. If dinos ate hamburgers, T. rex could have swallowed more than 2,000 in a single bite.

All of the T. rex fossils discovered have been found in North America. In 1990, one of the best-known and most complete skeletons was discovered in South Dakota by fossil hunter Sue Hendrickson. In October 1997, the Field Museum in Chicago, Illinois, bought the bones for a record $8.4 million. The fossil, known simply as "Sue," is now on display for all visitors to look at.

# DISCUSSION QUESTIONS

1. Ben took David's time machine controller without permission. If you were David, would you forgive Ben for taking the remote? Why or why not?

2. In the story, Ben and Darrin help David stop the T. rex. Do you think David could have stopped the T. rex by himself? Explain your answer.

3. Do you think making Brendan pay back the money he took is a good punishment? How would you have punished Brendan for bringing back the T. rex?

# WRITING PROMPTS

1. Robo-Dog 3000 was a pretty strange pet. Write a story about your favorite pet. If you don't have one, describe your dream pet. Would it be a robot, a wild animal, or something even crazier?

2. If you had a time machine would you travel to the past or the future? Write a story about the places you would go and the adventures you would have.

3. T. rex and the triceratops are just two types of dinosaurs. Ask an adult to help you find information about another dinosaur or extinct animal. Describe what it looked like, where it lived, and what it ate.